Through the Year With Gertrude Grosbeak

Written and Illustrated by Meg Lowman

the Peppertree Press
Sarasota, Florida

Happy birthday, Mom

Copyright © Margaret Lowman, 2016

All rights reserved. Published by the Peppertree Press, LLC.
The Peppertree Press and associated logos are trademarks of the Peppertree Press, LLC.

No part of this publication may be reproduced, stored in a retrieval system, transmitted in any form or by any means, electronic, mechanical, photocopying, recording, or otherwise, without prior written permission of the publisher and author/illustrator. Graphic design by Rebecca Barbier.

For information regarding permission,
call 941-922-2662 or contact us at our website:
www.peppertreepublishing.com or write to:
the Peppertree Press, LLC.
Attention: Publisher
1269 First Street, Suite 7
Sarasota, Florida 34236

ISBN: 978-1-61493-459-2

Library of Congress Number: 2016908776

Printed July 2016

As a child, I loved nature. My friends teased me and I was definitely the class "nerd for nature!" I loved birds at a young age, and had my very own field guide plus a cheap pair of binoculars. I remember seeing the Grosbeaks at our bird feeder one winter, and hatched the story of Gertrude Grosbeak. At the age of 9, I learned to use the rickety old family Remington typewriter. One day, I typed the story of Gertrude Grosbeak and other birds that I had come to know and love at our family bird feeder in the winter.

This book sat in my mom's closet for the next 50 years, and now I am publishing it as a surprise gift for her 88th birthday. -- and thanks for not only saving this manuscript, but also taking me bird watching on many early (and chilly) childhood mornings.

A few years after Gertrude was "born," I took my wildflower collection (I had 100s pressed in telephone books) and entered the 5th grade state science fair. Standing among almost 500 boys (many with their volcano experiments), I was humbled that my pressed flowers won 2nd prize in the New York State Science Fair. Although it did not appear to me that the world welcomed girls in science, I was inspired by my bird-watching and my wild-flowers to pursue my love for the natural world.

—Dr. Margaret Lowman

The author at her 5th grade Science Fair

Chapter 1
The New Year's Eve Party

"Where's my polka-dot dress? I am always losing my dress!" cried Gertrude Grosbeak to her best friend, Wilma Woodpecker, as Wilma was putting on her red cap.

"Now, let's see," said Wilma, "You loaned your speckled dress to Mrs. Woodthrush and your red dress to Cornelia Cardinal, and your purple one to Mrs. Martin. That only leaves your blue dress with the red stripes. Had you forgotten that you took your polka-dot dress to the laundry?"

Gertrude Grosbeak and Wilma Woodpecker share an apartment on Sapsucker Drive in Nuthatch Village. They are always getting mixed up. Finally, Gertrude and Wilma left for the party. Wilma drove the bird-o-copter. By the time they reached Mr. Flicker's house, Gertrude had smoothed her ruffled feathers.

The first game they played at the New Year's Eve party was PIN-THE-BEAK-ON-THE-BIRD. Every time someone tried to pin the beak, Gertrude rushed up to look. But when Jenny Wren had her turn, Wilma looked a little too long and she got pinned right on her ruffled feathers. "OOOOUCH!" she screamed (mostly with surprise, but not pain).

When it was time to eat, they had rose wine in acorns. The main course was sunflower seeds cooked in mushroom sauce. Then came dessert, the best course of all. Whoever found a tiny horseshoe in his bluejay turnover got a prize. Wouldn't you know! Gertrude Grosbeak found a horseshoe in her turnover. Guess what the prize was? A pair of red wood socks for winter wear. "Oh, how delightful!!" squealed Gertrude. "They will go well with my new outfit I ordered in the Catbird Country Store catalog. And they will be just right when I go skating on frozen bird baths."

Gertrude and Wilma got home late. They were so tired they went right to bed and had many bird dreams.

Chapter 2
Gertrude Uses the Washing Machine

The next day while Gertrude was outside looking at her prize socks (because she thought they were beautiful), she happened to drop them in the mud. "Oh dear!" cried Gertrude. She took the wool socks down to the washing machine. Gertrude did not know how to operate the machine, but what did she care! Just so her new socks got clean!

She turned on a dial. Later she looked at the washing machine. "Hmmmmm, it seems as if it's not working, Gertrude Grosbeak mumbled. So she turned three more dials and put the socks into the machine. A half hour later Gertrude went down to check her socks. She poked her head into the machine but could not see anything. She looked again and finally saw two red specks. She pulled them out. They were Gertrude's socks, all right. "They must have shrunk," Gertrude sadly observed. (Wool does shrink in hot water!)

When Wilma heard about the socks she laughed and laughed. Gertrude wanted to wear the socks anyways. So she wore them on her middle toes.

If you ever happen to see a Grosbeak with a red middle toe, you will know who it is. IT'S GERTRUDE!!

Chapter 3
The Trip to Hawaii

If there was anything Gertrude liked better than banana ice-cream with butterscotch sauce, cottage cheese, a cherry and a sprig of parsley on top (with peanut butter sandwiches on the side), it was contests. Gertrude LOVED contests. She joined contests to win trips, cars, toys, books, animals or anything else, even though she never won.

One day there was a contest. The prize was a trip to Hawaii. Gertrude joined as usual. To enter the contest she wrote a poem about traveling. Here it is:

I'd like to see Hawaii and its shores of golden sand.

I'd like to see pineapple plants. Wouldn't it be grand?

I'd dance the Hula-hula on a shiny moonlit night,
And swim in the ocean waters when the sun is bright.

By golly, Gertrude won the Contest, a trip to Hawaii for two! Wilma Woodpecker and Gertrude Grosbeak set off for Hawaii on a Robinjet 747. When they reached Honolulu (the capital of Hawaii), the first thing Gertrude wanted to do was learn the Hula dance. You should have seen her try! She couldn't do it very well, but she had fun. Grosbeak hips just do not seem to wiggle!

Later they went to a restaurant for pigeon pie, Nuthatch salad and crabapple tarts. Then they went to their room at the Vireo Hotel and planned a big day ahead.

Chapter 4
The Train Ride

One day when Gertrude went downstairs to get the Bird Gazette she saw an article that caught her eye. It said there was going to be a World's Fair in New York City. "What a good time to visit Grandmother and Grandfather Grosbeak," thought Gertrude. She wrote a letter to her Grandmother and asked if she could visit. Gertrude got a letter back saying that her grandparents would be delighted to see her.

When Gertrude got on the train bound for New York City, she looked around for some other birds to sit with. She did not see any and went up to the conductor. "Could you please tell me where I can find the birds?" she asked. The conductor laughed, and said "This is a People's train, not a bird train."

Gertrude replied, "But my ticket says this train is called the PHOEBE SNOW," says Gertrude. She felt embarrassed walking back to her seat. "No wonder everyone is staring at me," she said to herself. The conductor was still laughing.

She arrived in New York City safety and met her Grandmother. They went home and had pizza pie with her Grandfather. The next day Gertrude went to the World's Fair. What sights she saw! She looked at herself in a queer mirrors and thought she had better go on a diet! She stopped to see a dinosaur exhibit and screamed with fright, thinking they were real. She enjoyed seeing the cars of the future and pledged to start driving lessons when she got home. She tried to imagine herself in a modern jet-propelled car.

It was finally time for Gertrude to return home. She thanked her grandparents for the nice time and left on the Phoebe Snow Train. When she disembarked from the train in her home town, she heard the conductor say, "Whew! She is the first passenger we ever had to order Nasturtium Seed soup in the diner car!"

Chapter 5
A Sticky Mess

Gertrude had nothing to do one afternoon, so she decided to bake something. She found a recipe for Marshmallow Treat. She took out the eggs, flour, milk, sugar, butter and marshmallows. She mixed them according to the directions, put them into a greased pan and popped them into the oven. In 45 minutes, Gertrude went into the kitchen to get her Marshmallow Treat out of the oven. When she saw them, they looked the same as before. "Now what on earth did I do wrong?" she stammered. She looked around and then remembered she did not turn on the oven! Gertrude noticed the directions said not to let the batter stand for too long or it will get very sticky. "Oh well, it won't matter," she said to herself as she put them back into the oven. In 45 minutes, Gertrude took out the marshamallow treat. She tried cutting it. It stuck to the knife. She put her hand in the dish so she could break it into chunks. It stuck to her fingers. Gertrude was plum stuck up!!!

Luckily it had rained that day and she managed to soak most of the sticky mess from her feathers. But she is still plucking the batter from her feathers now and then. If you see a grosbeak who is plucking at her wings, you will know it is Gertrude.

Chapter 6
Gertrude Has a Sale

"We don't need all these hats and pants. We can't even use these toys," Wilma Woodpecker exclaimed to Gertrude Grosbeak. "Why don't we have a sale?" Gertrude suggested. "Why, that is a wonderful idea!" Wilma replied. So they decided to have a yard sale.

Gertrude had just finished folding the clothes when an idea struck her. She could also sell the sticky surprise (for it was ONLY 4 days old!) for glue. Gertrude put it in plastic bottles and added a little water. She put the bottles on a table beside her Sweet Song Cure Medicine and put up a sign that looked like this:

The birds came gradually. Many things were sold. Mr. and Mrs. Mockingbird bought a pair of ski socks, a blouse, a china set, a people book and a toy teddybear. There was a great chatter over the "Sweet Song Cure Medicine" and also the "Sticky Surprise Drops." Soon they were both sold out. Gertrude was so surprised that she blushed! The sale was a success and afterward she and Wilma celebrated by having some mince-meat and cider.

Step Right UP!
Get some Sweet Song Cure Medicine. It "Tames a trill," cures a warble!
Sticky Surprise Drops
1 drop to brighten your feathers or use it as glue!

Chapter 7
Gertrude Wins a Medal

Gertrude had a hobby. It was license plates. She tried to copy and memorize the license plate of every car she saw, just for fun. If she had time she would draw the car and write its color. One day when Gertrude was on Main Street she saw a different kind of car. She thought it was interesting so she drew the car and wrote down its color and license.

That night as Gertrude skimmed through the "Bird Gazette" newspaper, she saw an article about a big robbery. "Robbery! Twelve thousand dollars and jewels were stolen!" exclaimed Gertrude. She read a description of what the police thought was the robbers' getaway car. "If anyone knows the license of this car, please report to our nearest police station," she read aloud. Gertrude got excited by that! She loved detective work, so she decided to look through her collection of license numbers. She looked through quite a few and some car illustrations she had drawn, but none was quite right.

Suddenly, Gertrude came to one that matched the description. She was all excited. She clipped the story out of the newspaper and took her illustration to the police office. There she met Chief Cardinal. He was thrilled and amazed at the accuracy of Gertrude's drawings. "You have solved our case!" said the Chief. Gertrude was overwhelmed with joy.

The police captured the robbers. That night there was a big report about Gertrude in the newspaper. It told about her life and her license plate hobby. The next day there were many bird women and birdmen on Greenclover Field. They had come to see Gertrude receive her award. The Mayor of the town made a speech and then he pinned a medal on Gertrude! She beamed with birdly pride. When the ceremony was over, Gertrude came home to bed, and had many pleasant bird dreams.

Chapter 8
Gertrude Loves Science

It was a lovely day. When Gertrude woke up she could hear Wilma chattering over a spilled bottle of milk. Gertrude and Wilma always filled their milk bottles about one-fourth full, because Wilma always had a habit of dropping things. She did not like to hold cold things in early morning because she got "wing fever." Gertrude got dressed and had her breakfast of bird-seed oatmeal, sliced cherries, seed toast and a glass of morning dew.

Gertrude decided to work in her laboratory. She wanted to join the Science Club and was working on an invention that would be useful to birds and also to people. She had come up with something, a burglar catcher to put in your room at night. This is how it worked:

You hear the burglar.

You press the button on the machine. A hand comes out with a ball on it. When the hand touches the floor, it shoots the ball up. A bow and arrow shoots the

ball. Then a ball rolls down a chute and hits a small garbage can. That scares the burglar!

The burglar runs but he slips on a cake of soap which comes sliding along the floor.

Meanwhile, a machine in the ball starts making noise.

The scared burglar doesn't move. The big ball rolls over him and the robot ties him up with rope.

Then you turn the machine off and press a button that calls the police station.

When Gertrude registered her invention at the Science Club (so she might be accepted as a member), everyone laughed. But she proved the machine really worked, using Professor Starling as her victim. Gertrude was given her full membership papers. She donated the machine to the police. They don't seem to use Gertrude's invention too much but every bird visitor asks to see how it works. If you ever hear any chattering birds in the woods they are probably laughing at Gertrude's invention.

Chapter 9
The End of the Bird's Tail (Tale)

"Oh dear, I forgot to go to the grocery store," said Gertrude over the Be Kind to Whooping Crane Weekend. (Whooping cranes are endangered, and close to extinction.)

"You can't go now because all the stores are closed. We don't have any birdseed, honeydew or milk," exclaimed Wilma. The special weekend was very important to the bird world, so that all creatures would be aware of the importance of all bird species.

"I'll go to the bird feeder at the people's house," replied Gertrude.

"Bring enough for 3 meals!" said Wilma.

Because it was so nice outside, Gertrude decided not to take the birdocopter. When she reached the house she flew to the bird feeder on a window ledge. Inside the window there was a little girl in bed. Gertrude had seen here there many times and wondered what could be wrong. Gertrude got birdseed that would last for the day and flew off.

The next morning, Gertrude came for birdseed again. The window was open and Gertrude hopped

in and started chattering (in bird language) with the girl. Over by the little girl's bed there was a bird cage. Gertrude flew in, took a sip of the water, and nibble a few of the seeds. They were delicious! "I would almost like to live here," Gertrude thought. She took some seed for Wilma and went home.

Next week a letter came for Wilma. It was from Wilma's mother. She wanted Wilma to come and live with her and help take care of her. Gertrude said, "Oh Wilma, you should go. I'll be all right and I think I know just the spot for me, a place where I am needed.

"If you think I should go, I suppose I should," Wilma said sadly but excitedly.

In the next 3 weeks there was a clutter and commotion in Wilma and Gertrude's house. Gertrude found a small suitcase and packed all of her things in it. Wilma sent off a trunk by Bird Express. Before they left, Mrs. Nuthatch had a surprise party for them. The neighbors gave Wilma and Gertrude each a bottle of honeydew nectar.

Wilma left the next day. Then came the day for Gertrude to fly away. She put on her polka-dot dress, a sun bonnet, and her new turquoise beads. Gertrude did not tell anyone where she was going, especially Wilma.

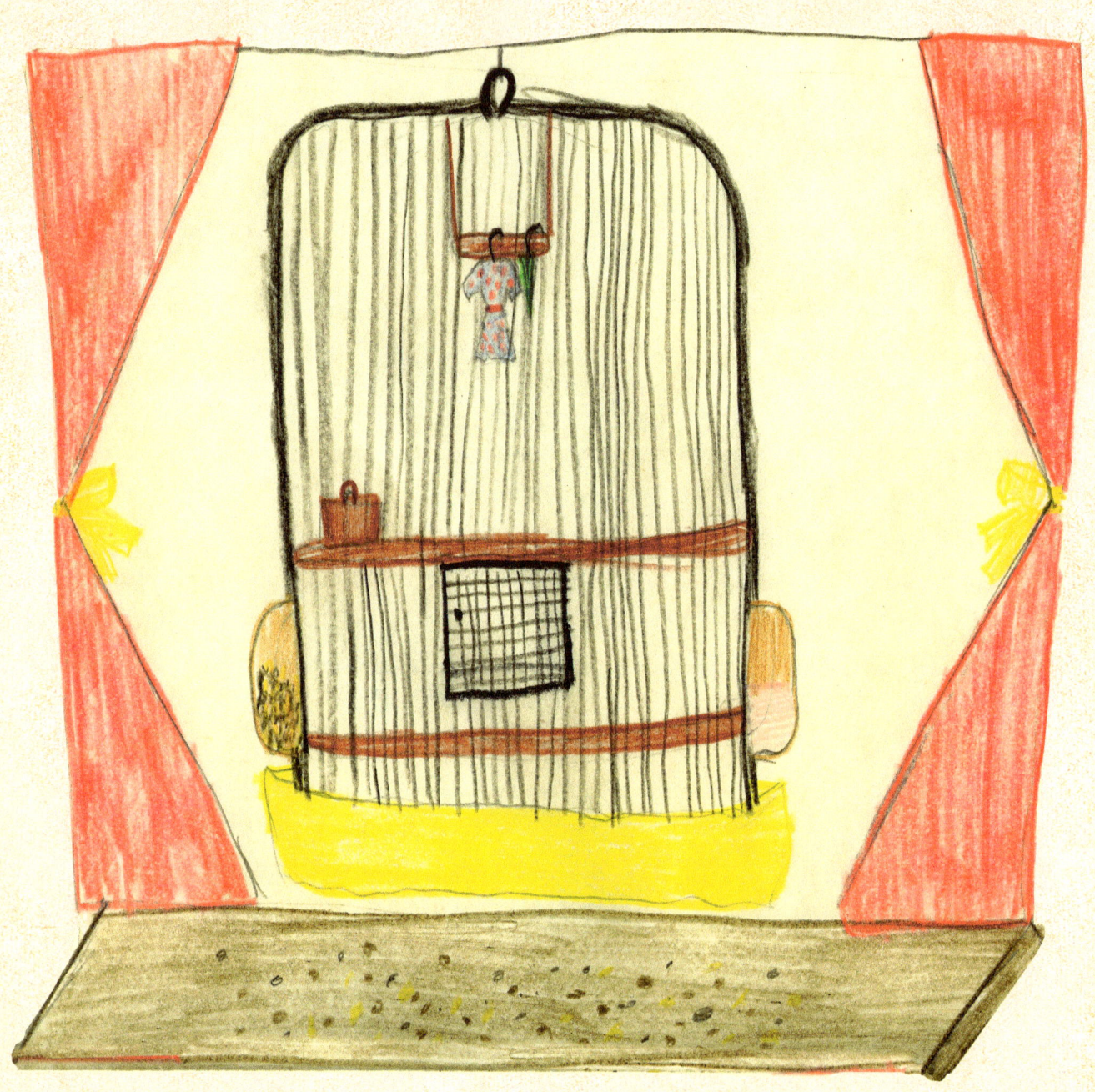

When she reached the little girl's house, the window was open and Gertrude went right in and hopped into the bird cage. The little girl giggled for she had NEVER seen a bird wear clothes. The little girl's eyes looked happy (for the first time in many months). She seemed to know that Gertrude would stay. From that day on, Gertrude lived with the little girl. The bird cage was always open so Gertrude could exercise her wings (for she was a wild bird, after all). Gertrude and her new friends had great times together. Whenever the little girls started talking, Gertrude would chatter and start a conversation in her own language. This always brought a smile or two from the little girl. The reason she stayed in bed was because she was unable to walk after an accident. Gertrude always had a way to cheer her up and brighten her day.

The birds of Nuthatch Village missed Gertrude. Whenever any birds came to the little girl's window feeder, they would peek inside. Sometimes they saw a Grosbeak in the cage. One of the cardinals was sure he had spotted a small polka dot dress hanging on the cage's swing.

"My, my," the birds would all wonder, "Do you suppose that could be Gertrude?"

The End

CPSIA information can be obtained
at www.ICGtesting.com
Printed in the USA
BVHW021501031221
622998BV00002B/56